Parents and Caregivers,

Stone Arch Readers are designed to provide enjoyable reading experiences, as well as opportunities to develop vocabulary, literacy skills, and comprehension. Here are a few ways to support your beginning reader:

- Talk with your child about the ideas addressed in the story.

- Discuss each illustration, mentioning the characters, where they are, and what they are doing.

- Read with expression, pointing to each word. You may want to read the whole story through and then revisit parts of the story to ensure that the meanings of words or phrases are understood.

- Talk about why the character did what he or she did and what your child would do in that situation.

- Help your child connect with characters and events in the story.

Remember, reading with your child should be fun, not forced. Each moment spent reading with your child is a priceless investment in his or her literacy life.

Gail Saunders-Smith, Ph.D.

STONE ARCH READERS

are published by Stone Arch Books, a Capstone Imprint
1710 Roe Crest Drive
North Mankato, Minnesota 56003
www.capstonepub.com

Library of Congress Cataloging-in-Publication Data
Klein, Adria F. (Adria Fay), 1947–
The full freight train / by Adria Klein ; illustrated by Craig Cameron.
p. cm. -- (Stone Arch readers: Train time)
Summary: Freight Train is carrying bananas, tomatoes, apples, and potatoes.
ISBN 978-1-4342-4784-1 (library binding) -- ISBN 978-1-4342-6197-7 (pbk.)
1. Railroad trains--Juvenile fiction. [1. Railroad trains--Fiction. 2. Color--Fiction.]
I. Cameron, Craig, ill. II. Title.
PZ7.K678324Ful 2013
[E]--dc23   2012046960

Reading Consultants:
Gail Saunders-Smith, Ph.D.
Melinda Melton Crow, M.Ed.
Laurie K. Holland, Media Specialist
Designer: Russell Griesmer

Printed in China by Nordica.
0413/CA21300452
032013   007226NORDF13

The Full Freight Train

illustrated by
Craig Cameron

written by
Adria F. Klein

STONE ARCH BOOKS
a capstone imprint

Freight Train was full.

"I have a lot of food," he said.

Freight Train went to town.

He stopped at the train station.

"Time to unload," he said.

Take off the red tomatoes.

Take off the orange carrots.

Take off the yellow bananas.

Take off the green beans.

Take off the brown potatoes.

"Now I am empty," said
Freight Train.

"But we are full," the people said.

"Thank you, Freight Train!"

Toot! Toot!

STORY WORDS

station   tomatoes   bananas

unload   carrots   potatoes

Word Count: 73

STONE ARCH READERS   LEVEL 1
Big Train Takes a Trip
written by
Adria F. Klein
illustrated by
Craig Cameron

STONE ARCH READERS   LEVEL 1
Circus Train and the Clowns
written by
Adria F. Klein
illustrated by
Craig Cameron

STONE ARCH READERS   LEVEL 1
City Train in Trouble
written by
Adria F. Klein
illustrated by
Craig Cameron